One Hell of a Road Trip

C.H. Lyn

Horizon Publishing

Contents

Other Works by C.H. Lyn

Spooky Cat

Love is Murder

<u>The Abredea Series</u>
Hope and Lies
Truth and Fury

<u>Miss Belle's Travel Guides</u>
Lacey Goes to Tokyo
Damen Goes to Peru

<u>The Old Tales</u>
Song of the Deep
A Voice in the Tower

Author Disclaimer:

Hey friends! My version of differentiating between witch and wiccan in this story is purely for the story – absolutely fictional – and not at all a reflection of real-world magic users. I have many wiccan and witchy friends, and I want to ensure no one feels hurt because of the verbiage and portrayal in this story.

One

Preparing for a road trip is a tricky procedure. Having to bear in mind that a demon who guards a gate of hell is constantly on the hunt for one of your best friends while preparing for a road trip, is harder.

Add on the fact that we're bringing my tiny black cat and we're on a time crunch and the "relaxing time away from the city" that Agatha promised is looking more and more like a stressful next week and a half.

. . . .

"I'm just saying," I utter through gritted teeth. "If I can't get these window shades to stick, it might make sense for you to stay home."

Skia, a shadowy demon who spent the last five-hundred years in hell, somehow narrows their eyes. How, no clue. My friend is the incarnation of demonic energy with no capsule. They often remind me of thick black smoke—if smoke was sentient.

Little red eyes squint at me. "*I'll not stay behind, Demi. This city is large, but I crave more. I dream of conquering the rest of this land.*"

I snort. At the trunk, Ags does the same. She pops her head up from where she's been Tetris-ing our luggage. Vibrant purple streaks in her hair shine in the faint beam of streetlight coming down a block away. It's hard to pack at night, but too much light hurts Skia.

Hence the window shades.

"Skia," Ags says, humor in her tone, "is 'conquering' the right word? Or do you mean seeing? Seeing the rest of this land is very different than conquering it."

Skia shifts, their shadowy body wrapped around the head-rest, to turn those beady eyes on Ags. "*I said what I meant.*"

"And when exactly did you conquer Denver?" I ask with a smirk on my lips. "I don't keep up on the news much; I must have missed it."

Ags lets out a barking laugh and shoves one last box into the trunk.

We wouldn't have as much crap in this little rental car, but we aren't just attending this wedding; Agatha is officiating it.

For traditional folks that would mean bringing some religious text and maybe a laptop. For Ags' cousin and her groom-to-be, it means Ags is lugging half of her witchy/wiccan gear to the east coast.

We also have to get there a day early to help set up.

None of which I mind. My issue stems from trying to stop Skia burning up in daylight while we are driving. And trying to stop Missy from flipping out and shredding her car carrier.

"*Problems for the morning, Demi.*" Skia murmurs, their voice in my mind only.

I sigh. With a grunt, I'm able to get the shade fixed into place, and I turn to my demonic friend. "How do you do that?"

The shadow bounces on the seat, a gesture I've taken to be a shrug. "*You aren't as hard to read as you think, my friend.*"

"Or you're in my head."

Skia scoffs. "*I'd never betray your trust in such a way.*"

I raise my eyebrows, crossing my arms with incredulity.

"*Well, and I can't use my power or the demons from hell will find me. Talking to you privately takes some of my own effort, but reading your mind is beyond my personal capacity.*"

This response is more believable. I know it to be true, and I'm glad Skia has been so careful. The thought of coming face to face with Nexus, a gate keeper of hell bent on dragging my friend back to the underworld, stirs snakes of anxiety in my gut. We went head-to-head once before. That was almost six months ago when Skia first arrived on this plane.

Missy and I sent Nexus back to hell empty handed—proving how smart cats are and guaranteeing that I have extradimensional enemies I never could have imagined before a demon possessed my cat.

Part of the ritual to banish Nexus also released Skia from the confines of Missy's body. Now I have two balls of black living in my studio apartment with me.

At least only one of them needs to use the litter box.

· · · ● · ● · ● · · · ·

"Double latte, americano, and two puppy cups."

The barista hands over our drinks. I thank her and am about to roll up the window when she asks, "I see one kitty, but where is the other one?"

A low hissing chuckle sounds from the floor of the back seat.

"The other one is shy," I reply with a smile.

In the passenger seat, comfortably tucked into a Buffy the Vampire Slayer blanket, Ags chuckles. I pass her the drinks, give the barista a nod, and pull away from the drive-thru.

We're on our way. Four days, over a dozen states, and several downloaded audio books and podcasts ready to go. I pull up the first campaign of NADDPOD (Not Another D&D Podcast) since Ags has yet to listen to it.

Skia moves under my seat, the edge of their shadow popping up between my legs, and I hand them a cup of whipped cream. *"Turn it up,"* they hiss. *"This is my favorite part."*

Missy yowls in agreement—or anger—until Ags tucks the second cup into her crate.

Two

My favorite part of the drive is early morning. I've got my coffee, low music, and there is minimal traffic. After a few hours, Ags takes over the driving and I focus on getting some homework done.

Was it Skia showing up that made me want to enroll in some online classes and start working towards my degree in World Religions? Maybe. Maybe it was explaining the whole situation to Ags, which led to her hanging around my apartment more. Which made my desire to have as little as possible to do with the outside world lessen—slightly.

Turns out human contact *is* important. I'm sure I'd be fine with just Skia and Missy, but as we blow past a billboard advertising Easter family dinners at some chain restaurant, I can't help the swell of gratitude I feel for Ags.

"Hey," I mutter. "Thanks for bringing us to this."

Agatha raises an immaculately penciled in eyebrow. When she had time to do them, I have no clue. We spent last night in a motel, and I'm pretty sure she was asleep until the very last moment possible this morning.

"Of course." She grins and glances into the backseat. Skia is beside Missy's crate, their shadowy form settled onto the cushions with an odd stretch of neck rising up so they can look out the shade-covered window. "Can't let Skia live without seeing more of the world, Demi."

Ags' gaze catches on me as she turns back to the road. I'm sure she's thinking the same thing about me. In the few years we've known each other she's never seen me leave the city.

I lean up against the door, enjoying the comfortability of this little rental. The view is stunning. Nonstop rolling hills, still green from the precipitation from winter. Flowers grow among the tall grass, dotting the landscape with color.

I used to live in a place like this.

I like the city.

• • • • ● • ● • • • •

Skia's favorite part of the drive is nighttime. I get behind the wheel again, and they sit on my lap, staring out the windshield with all the attention a new world deserves.

"*Why so many lights?*" they ask as we pull off the interstate and head toward our Airbnb.

I chuckle. "East coast. Big cities mean big lights."

"*And this... east coast... has many large metropolitan areas?*"

"Yeah. But there are plenty of places with more nature. We can find some hiking or something tomorrow."

I pull into the driveway of a petite house with a cute wrap-around porch and twinkling lights. Skia moves up onto my shoulder, away from the light coming in through my window.

"There have always been trees, Demi. I have less interest in nature and more in the marvels of humankind."

"That's... that's a really nice way to put it. We'll try to find some marvels for you."

Ags grins over at me. "That shouldn't be too hard, Skia. I have a few places in mind for us to visit tomorrow."

I raise an eyebrow as we step out of the car. "What places?"

She runs a hand through her dark hair with a chuckle. "Witchy places."

With no further explanation, and therefore leaving me completely bewildered, she grabs her overnight bag and head to the door to type in the code and let us all in.

I get Missy's crate from the back. She's done well so far, but she definitely prefers the solitude of her cushy box to the open air of the car. Skia slips into the big hood of my sweater, hanging down at the base of my neck. They flick my hair around and are soon entirely shrouded in darkness.

"Comfy back there?" I ask.

"Indeed."

"What are you going to do when I cut my hair?" I laugh, carrying us all into the cozy house. Skia weighs almost nothing, except when their wet. Oddly enough the shadow that makes up their form is really absorbent.

The low hiss of Skia's chuckle echoes in my mind as we go in, locate a take-out menu for a nearby pizza place, and order dinner.

"So," I mumble through a mouthful of pepperoni. "What witchy spot are we going to tomorrow? I thought we were in a bit of a hurry?"

Ags leans across the round dining table in the middle of the kitchen and grabs a slice of garlic bread. "We're a few hours from Salem."

I scrunch my nose, feeding a bit of pepperoni to Missy as she curls around my ankles. "Isn't that a *bad* place to be a witch?"

Ags rolls her eyes. "At one time, yes. Now, it's a tourist attraction. I think it'd be a fun spot. Plus, we might find something cute for my cousin. I'm not sold on the wine glasses I picked out."

"Surely not," Skia says, a slice of pizza disappearing into their shadowy form. *"It only took you two weeks to decide on that particular set."*

"And that was after you went with glasses instead of candlesticks," I add.

Ags gives us both a squinty glare. "Shaddup."

The three of us share a round of chuckles, and Missy yowls for more scraps.

"Salem it is," I say with a grin at my friends. "But if anyone lights any matches, we're outta there."

Three

Salem Massachusetts is an annoyingly beautiful town. For a place where so much awful stuff happened it's startlingly quaint.

Missy surprises me by staying on Ags' shoulder. She really adds to my friend's already highly witchy aesthetic. Flowing black skirts with violet and green embroidery, an "everyday" corset—as she calls them, thick eyeliner and mascara, and blood red lipstick already make her look like she walked out of a sequel to Practical Magic. Missy brings an element of mystery, and a touch of cuteness, to the whole ensemble.

Skia and I are a different story. I'm in my usual jeans and a comfy oversized sweater. Skia stirs fitfully in the big pocket. Bits of their form ooze out the sides, making it look like my hands are smoking. They shift around.

"Turn a bit, Demi. I want to see that."

I roll my eyes with a grin and move sideways so Skia can get a glimpse of the multi-passenger bike thing touristy places like this have.

"*They ride as one,*" Skia says.

A few steps ahead of me, Ags pauses to see what Skia is talking about. She cackles as the bike goes around a corner. "I've been on one of those before. Half of my cousins only pretended to pedal."

"*Ahh, falsifiers. They shall be rightly punished when their time on this plane ends.*"

I open my mouth, meet Ags' eye, and close it again. Skia has been here for a while now but still terrifies me with what they say half the time. Well, sort of terrifies. It's like watching a gruesome comedy. I often don't know if I should laugh or be utterly horrified.

"Nah." Ags spares me having to respond. "They're good guys. This was back when we were teenagers. Everyone's a dumbass as a teenager."

At this I do chuckle, nodding in agreement as Skia's head briefly pops out of my pocket to look up at me.

"*Your species is strange.*"

"Buddy, you have no idea." I glance up the street, and my heart swells at the site of a café sign a block away. "Coffee?"

Ags shakes her head, gently shifting Missy to her other shoulder. "You've gotta break this habit, Demi."

"No," I say with a grin, darting ahead of her as Skia hisses protests about being jostled. "I really don't."

. . . . ●. ● ● . . .

The coffee is hot, the pastry is fresh, and Skia is safely tucked behind me in the corner of our booth seat. The cold of their shadow caresses my shoulder as they eye my blueberry scone.

This little shop is as cute as the rest of the town. Lights hang at even intervals, casting shadows in odd shapes. If it weren't so crowded, I'd love to watch Skia dance through them like a cat burglar going through lasers. It's a game we play at home a lot.

But there are people at almost every table and the line is out the door.

Ags settles next to me after a five-minute wait for her drink, and she looks like she stepped in something rotten on the way over.

Missy jumps from her shoulder to also beg for pieces of my scone. I should have gotten two.

"What's wrong?" I wince as I sip the scolding coffee, but the warmth is so lovely as it spreads through my chest and belly that I care less about my slightly burnt tongue.

Ags shakes her head. With an angry expression still in place, she separates one of the many chains around her neck, pulling forth a purple crystal.

"Ags?" I prompt. I'm usually the one too distracted or spaced out to answer a question.

"That barista," she snaps.

I raise an eyebrow, noting the steam coming from Ags' mug. "It took a couple minutes, but your drink is still hot. What's the issue?"

Skia cocks the portion of shadow that is their head. "*Perhaps her scone is not as delectable as ours.*"

"Ours?" I scowl. "I specifically asked if you wanted anything before I ordered. You said no."

"*Hmph. I ought to try Agatha's scone. To check. Missy agrees.*"

My scowl becomes a snort as I break off a chunk of scone and raise it to my shoulder. It disappears from my fingers. Missy is next, and I give her a sizably smaller piece to avoid tummy issues later.

I think she notices, because when she kneads my leg her claws go deeper than usual.

Ags has ignored the entire conversation. She holds the crystal—amethyst, I think—to her lips and mutters against the stone.

"Ags, what's going on?"

"That woman is messed up."

I look to the front of the shop where the barista is laughing along with a customer about something.

"What happened?"

She shakes her head, finishes whatever chanting she was doing with the crystal, and lets it fall back to her chest. "She asked if I'm a witch."

I purse my lips, then lift my mug to avoid saying the wrong thing and wait for her to continue.

"That's not the problem." Ags flails a heavily ringed hand. "But when I told her I'm Wiccan she went off on me."

I frown. "That's crazy. Why?"

"She said Wiccans aren't real casters, and we're a white-washed version of witches and we give the whole magical community a bad name."

I sip my coffee.

For all the strange supernatural stuff I've seen since Skia possessed Missy, I have yet to witness any sort of human witchy/wiccan magic actually work.

Sure, there is manifesting what you want in life, there are candles that have scents to help someone relax, and I'm sure meditation is a beneficial part of the spell casting process. But actual magic? Like, lighting candles with a fingertip, or making things float, or any of the stuff seen in Hollywood... that's all continued to be fiction.

I don't say any of that to Ags. "That's a crazy thing to say to someone. Especially someone you don't know."

She nods, her cheeks still flushed.

"Umm, what *is* the difference between witch and wicca?" I ask tentatively.

"*Wiccans primarily use good magic. They work toward peace and generally avoid the darker curses and spells that would cause ruin.*"

Ags, who had opened her mouth to respond, stares at Skia. "That's true."

"*And witches have a history of aiming for power. They use whatever magic is at their disposal to get what they want, damn the consequences.*"

I nibble on my scone. "How do you know that?"

A feeling similar to a shrug. "*I spent a lot of time on earth back in the day. I've known my share of witches. And I pay attention when Ags does her rituals.*"

I flush, knowing full well that I do *not* pay attention when Ags gets her incense going around my apartment.

Ags sighs, her anger melting into a satisfied smile. "All of that is correct, Skia. So the idea that someone wants to claim being a witch, let alone scold me for being wiccan, is absolute garbage."

"Agreed." I look at the barista with new eyes, irritated at the way she's made my friend feel. "Well, now we know for the return trip."

Ags raises an eyebrow, and I grin.

"We'll find a different coffee shop when we head back home."

She shakes her head but laughs. On either side of me, tiny black creatures steal the last of my scone.

Four

We get one of those over-hyped tours after our coffee break. Ags holds a little notebook, jotting down information about her favorite spots so she can incorporate them into the map mural she wants to paint in her shop. It's going to be a large project with how many ideas she has, but I'm excited to help her get started.

I trail behind the rest of the tour group: Ags and Missy, a Dutch couple, and a handful of college students, to keep Skia out of sight. I'm a bit warm in my sweatshirt but taking it off requires finding a dark space to keep my demon pal out of the sun while I do it. In the meantime, Skia stirs restlessly as the tour guide stops yet again to point out another building.

This one might serve our purpose. The group strides into the red and white barn and wanders for a bit. I've spent my share of time in barns, and this one is clearly for tourism. The loft is far too clean, and the equipment is ancient.

The guide goes off on a spiel about the history of the building, and I duck out of the cluster of people following her. Skia and I head behind a line of old tractors, and I take off my sweater.

"Interesting."

Skia slides off my shoulder and into the scattered strands of too-clean hay.

"What?" I murmur. I bunch up the sweater so they can hide in the folds when we go back into the light.

"An old symbol," Skia says. *"I don't recall..."*

They swirl around, sending the hay to the side as though with a breeze, and reveal a black, painted pattern on the concrete floor.

"Looks like a pentagram." I crouch for a better look. It's similar enough to the five-pointed star, but there are added details that I don't recognize. Almost hieroglyphics.

"Not a pentagram." Skia's exasperation comes through the low hiss in my head. *"Something else."*

"Demi?"

I wave my hand at Skia, and they hurry back to the bundle in my arms. I stand and turn as Ags comes around the tractors with a raised eyebrow.

"Everyone is moving on."

"Yep, coming. Just had to take off my sweater." I gesture to the bundle of fabric and shadow in my arms and then follow Ags and the rest of the tour.

When the tour ends—and I have way too much information about burning women and the significance of mushrooms in my head—we make our way back to the little hostel we're staying in.

Ags booked us a private room with two beds. We fill up on bulky sandwiches and tea. Skia steals most of my ice cream, while Ags happily shares hers with Missy.

"Two days out," I say, stretching out on my bed and staring up at the popcorn ceiling. "You have your speech ready?"

She heaves a sigh. "Mostly. I want to talk to my cousin before I finalize everything. There should be plenty of time after we get there tomorrow."

"I'm here to help with all the set-up and stuff."

"*As am I.*"

Ags grins as she takes out her earrings and removes the excess of chains around her neck. "I appreciate it, both of you."

Missy, never one to be excluded, jumps onto the little vanity in front of Ags and gives a little yowl.

"Yes." Ags gives Missy scratches behind her ear. "You're a big help too."

I sit up a bit, looking over at my little black cat. "She seems..."

"Smarter?"

"Yeah, more intelligent since everything with Skia."

"*You're welcome.*"

I shake my head with half a chuckle as Skia darts around the shadows in the room to get near the vanity as well. Missy jumps down, and Skia clings to her back as she snakes under Ags' bed.

Ags meets my gaze. "She is though. It's a little eerie."

At this I let out a snort. "I mean, she was possessed by a demon. It doesn't get much eerier than that, does it?"

"Fair point," Ags cackles.

She finishes removing her plethora of make-up and rubs some sort of eucalyptus smelling lotion on her face. We turn down the lights so Skia and Missy can join us on my bed, and the four of us settle in for an episode of New Girl before bed. We were binging Supernatural for a little bit, but I got tired of the constant comments about what they got wrong about demons.

Missy is asleep before the episode ends. Skia curls up beside her, their textures the only way to distinguish where one ends and the other begins.

Ags goes to her bed and turns out the light, leaving only a beam of moonlight coming through the thin curtains of the window. She shifts for a few minutes before settling, and soon her steady deep breathing tells me she's asleep.

I roll onto my side, absentmindedly stroking Missy a few times. I think back to a year ago, cooped up in my apartment with such limited human contact that I almost thought I was a ghost a few times. Missy was my only companion for a long time. As hard as Ags tried to get me out of my shell, out of my own head, I wasn't ready.

Not until Skia came along.

I smile as the little shadow shifts. A low hissing murmur fills the room as they talk in their sleep.

The wedding will be fun. An opportunity to meet some new people and get dressed up. It took me forever to pick out the gray suit I brought. It's a little drab for this kind of wedding—so said Ags at the store—but I have a rainbow swirl pocket square and tie to spruce it up.

A flash of excitement burns through my chest. I haven't worn anything fancy in years, and the last time it wasn't exactly a set of clothes I was comfortable in.

I fade to sleep thinking of silly dances, champaign, and wedding cake.

Five

A crash of glass wakes me, but I can't move. Fear grips my chest, my stomach, and my heart. My eyes are open, but they are the only part of my body I can control. The only part obeying my commands.

The realization that it is still night, that moonlight is what pours in from the broken window just within my vision, scares me even more.

Someone broke in.

I strain every fiber of my being as a form moves toward me through the dark. I manage a grunt, my vocal cords finally uttering a fraction of the screams and curses going through my mind.

Hands—leather gloves imprinted with small symbols that shine with a silver glow in the moonlight—reach toward me.

No. Not toward *me*. My gaze, which I hope is showing my fury rather than my fear, follows the figure as they reach beside me and come away with a soft black shadow tight in their grasp.

Tiny red eyes glint for a brief second. They met mine. Betrayal, fear, pain, all clear as day on the not-quite-a-face of my friend.

I can't explain. Can't speak beyond another furious grunt as the figure clutching Skia backs toward the window. Unintelligible words are exchanged. Not with my friend. With someone outside.

Another glint of light shows some kind of cage. Metal, gold maybe, though it's impossible to tell from my prone position. I finally hear Skia, a faint sound in the back of my head, barely audible.

"Demi? What's going—"

Skia's soft hiss fades out and a retching, aching fury slams through my chest. I move. The muscles in my back shift. My fingers twitch.

I rise a few inches off the pillow, teeth gritted with effort.

The figure at the window turns to me, their hood too deep to make out any features. They raise their hand and snap their fingers.

Everything goes dark.

· · · ● · ● · ● · · ·

I come to with a jolt. Frantically flailing every limb to make sure they work; I practically fall out of bed. Sweat drenches me. Fury radiates through my still foggy head.

"Demi?"

I spin, whipping blankets off of me. Ags is just sitting up, blinking blearily and frowning in confusion.

"I had the strangest dream..."

A gust of cool air cuts off her words, and the two of us turn to the window. The broken window with a faint slip of moonlight glinting on shattered glass.

"Skia."

My voice trembles. I lunge from the bed, sprinting to the pair of jeans I slung over the back of a chair before going to sleep. I tug them on, dragging a sweater over my head as I try to shake through my gut-clenching fear and think.

Broken glass crunches underneath my thick socks.

"Demi," Ags says as she scrambles from her bed as well. "Careful."

I nod without looking at her and dust glass off the soles of my feet before pulling on my boots. A shard nicks my hand, but I barely notice. "What was that?" I ask, my tone not as sturdy as I'd like. "Why couldn't we move?"

"I thought..." Ags winces. She's moving almost as fast as I am, tugging on a cardigan and her shoes. "I thought it was a dream."

"Not a dream," I grunt. "Skia is gone."

I hesitate, a thought making my blood run cold.

"Missy?"

Ags blanches. She turns around the room and calls out for the cat as well. "Missy, come out sweetie."

Nothing moves. I blink back tears. "Why would someone take them? How long were we asleep again after—"

"Not long," Ags interrupts, shaking her head. She strides toward the door.

"How do you know?"

She points to an old-fashioned clock on the wall across from the window. "That's about all I could see from where I was. It's only been half an hour."

Relief hits me and is immediately doubled by a yowling from the open window.

I hurry toward the panes of broken glass. "Missy."

I expect her to leap into my arms, or at least tread carefully back into the room. Instead, she paces along the ground, glares those yellow eyes up at me, and yowls again.

Ags follows me to the window. She meets my eye. "Maybe she…"

"Knows where they took Skia, yeah."

I dart away from the window to snatch the keys off the dresser.

"What are we going to—"

"Get Skia back," I snap, my voice harsher than I mean it to be. I look at Ags, suck in a breath, and try again. "We're going to get Skia back."

The understanding shining through her eyes is part of why I value her friendship so much. She nods.

I look at my cat. "We're going through the door. Meet you in a second."

I swear Missy rolls her eyes, but I'm in too much of a hurry to think about that very hard. Within a minute Ags and I are standing outside the window of our room. A brief concern about how much that's going to cost to replace plays through my mind—a reprieve from the worry eating through me about what is happening to Skia.

Missy darts forward as we arrive, rubs against my shin for half a second, and then scampers into the darkness.

"Good thing I charged my phone," Ags mutters. She pulls up her flashlight app and the two of us hurry into the night after a very small, very black cat.

23

We move through tall grass for a while. The cuffs of my pants grow damp. It must be early morning with the amount of dew on the ground and the soft gray light edging the horizon.

There is something reassuring in following Missy. She does not amble. She has purpose, a destination she's leading us to. Worry still gnaws at me as the sun gets closer to rising.

If the monsters who took Skia from us are outside when the sun comes up...

"How much further do you think?" Ags' voice is a comforting reprieve from my own thoughts.

I'm about to respond when Missy darts out of the brush. We follow her onto an empty sidewalk and street. My eyes widen.

"Weren't we just here?"

Ags nods. "Main street. This is so strange."

I follow her gaze to a building a few yards down the road. Missy moves towards it, creeping with her front half close to the ground as though she's on the hunt. Even in the dim light, the red and white paint is visible.

"Is that the barn?"

I glance back the way we came and shake my head. Our hostel is only a few blocks away.

Missy pauses. She looks back at us, and her yellow eyes narrow.

"Coming," I whisper.

She waits for us to reach her, then paws my ankle and leads the way closer to the barn. Voices sound from inside, muffled and low but audible with how quiet the street is.

We crouch and move along the side of the barn as silently as possible.

There are wide windows at the top. They likely lead to the hay loft. The rear side of the building—our side—has a massive sliding door, but we have no idea what's inside. Or if the door is locked or barred.

Ags points up and mouths, "Window?"

I frown, chest tight with unease. A ladder. We need a ladder.

A hiss draws my attention. Missy sits a few yards away behind the next-door building. Her paw rests on a rusty-looking ladder.

I hurry to her. "You're getting creepy, you know that?" I whisper.

She says nothing as I heft the ladder. Of course, she's a cat.

I shake my head a little. Missy's super-cat intelligence is something to think about another time.

I return to Ags, who has been leaning with her ear against the wall to the barn.

"They definitely have Skia in there," she practically breathes. She backs away, taking a scrunchy from her wrist and tying her long dark hair into a bun.

"This is going to make some kind of noise." I jerk my head at the ladder. "But we *need* to get in there and see what's going on."

Ags nods, chewing on her bottom lip. "I'll go to the street. Slam something? Maybe break a window?"

I swallow. That doesn't feel like enough yet also seems like too much. "I have another idea."

I set the ladder down and take off my sweater. With quick movements I tie the fabric around one of the top ends of the ladder. A bit of cloth snags on the cut on my hand and pulls. I grit my teeth as the skin opens more, blood oozing out. I wipe it on my pants.

Ags, seeing my intention with the ladder, quickly pulls off her cardigan and hands it over. I muffle the other side.

It's our luck the high window is already open. Something tells me they don't bother closing it unless there is bad weather, which also makes me worried there will be a bunch of sleeping birds in the too-clean hay up there.

Not that we have much of a choice.

Ags holds one side of the ladder, and I clench my fingers around the other. Sweating with effort and tension, we bring it down gently on the window ledge. There is a soft thump, barely louder than dropping rolled up socks onto carpet.

I take another moment to appreciate Agatha. She's stout and strong, a fair contrast to my thin frame. Without her help easing the top of the ladder down, I'd have made a ton of noise.

I hold my breath for a few seconds, listening hard. Ags' eyes are as wide as mine, fixed on the wood panels in front of us as though if she concentrates hard enough, she'll be able to hear through them.

My heart continues to thunder, but there is no more waiting. I crouch and pat my shoulder. Missy takes a deep breath, then launches onto her usual perch. With her tail curled around the back of my neck, I begin to climb.

· · · ● · ● · ● · · · ·

"I don't understand the confusion. You're meant to be intelligent creatures, yet my words are lost in the mundane delusion and ineptitude you possess."

I never imagined the scathing sound of pissed-off Skia would be so comforting.

Ags and I crouch at edge of the hay loft. We crawled, staying low and grateful for the lack of creaking wood beneath us as we moved slowly toward the sounds of voices.

Four cloaked figures stand beneath us. They're surrounding a golden cage, set upon the center of the not-pentagram Skia and I noticed yesterday. A ton of candles have me itching to call the fire department, and the strong scent of rotten meat hangs in the air.

That won't be good for the tours.

My muscles tense at the response from the people below us.

"You're in our possession now, demon." One of the figures whips back their hood, and Ags practically vibrates with anger beside me.

It's the woman from the coffee shop, the barista who claimed to be a witch. Well, I guess she is a witch given the set-up downstairs.

Her hair is down, dark curls falling around her face. Her expression is obscured from our vantage point, but I can picture the scornful look that probably accompanies her tone.

"*Possession?*" Skia laughs, the sound sending a chill up my spine. "*You know nothing of possession. You're children, all of you. Playing at things you don't understand.*"

A chuckle goes through the group.

"Oh, we understand." Another hood comes down, revealing a blonde woman with twin braids and heavy make-up. Sort of a preppy version of Wednesday Adams. "You're a demon. You have power beyond measure. Power mankind can only dream of."

I cock my head, an incredulous squint in my eye as I recall the way Nexus almost killed us in my apartment. Skia certainly has power. They stopped a handful of assholes jumping me in an alley. But compared to a gatekeeper from hell, they aren't exactly high up on the food chain.

The woman continues. "Power *we* want."

Skia gives an unmistakable, hissing, snort. They respond, the words fading into the back of my mind as a plan grows in my mind.

I pull out my phone, make sure it's on silent, and gesture for Ags to do the same. There is no danger of being overheard if we are texting each other.

Missy brushes against my leg, rubbing her head into my arm as though telling me I need to get on with it. I give a few reassuring scratches behind her ear and return to sending the plan to Ags.

Seven

"**Y**ou *will* grant us your power."

The conversation between Skia and four witches has been going on at least five minutes now. It's clear these women didn't have an entire plan formulated before they took my demon friend.

I am curious why Skia hasn't simply slid through the golden wires of the cage surrounding them, but there must be some reason. Possibly something to do with why they didn't melt out of the gloved hand that took them in the first place.

The increasing strain of Skia's voice tells me this they aren't staying to play some twisted game to teach the witches a lesson.

"*What part of* I can't use my demonic abilities *are you struggling to understand?*" they hiss with growing frustration.

The blonde witch, who appears to be leading the group, snarls. "We captured you. According to the texts—"

"*What texts?*" Skia demands. "*Words written by humans? They mean nothing.*"

I glance at the window behind me. Ags is gone, headed to the car we left in front of our hostel. I'd thought about trying to get further up the coast yesterday, but now I'm glad we stayed in Salem. Though, maybe if we'd left town these witches wouldn't have stolen Skia.

"If you can't give us what we want, you'll have to contact someone who can."

"*...What?*"

My chest tightens at the fear in Skia's tone.

"Yeah," another witch, with a flaming red and orange pixie cut, says. "You do look pretty small. We want something more."

"*I'm not sure what you mean.*"

The polite way Skia hisses across the minds of everyone here is scarier than when they are angry. I shift, moving across the hayloft for a better view of the golden cage my friend is trapped in.

"You have a way to contact hell."

It isn't stated like a question, but Skia's silence seems to irritate the witches. One steps forward with a small black object in their hand.

My spine tingles with apprehension. I suck in a breath as the woman presses the object through the bars of Skia's cage.

It's a taser.

I have to bite back the shriek of rage that wants to leap from my throat as an electric charge goes through the cage. Skia's shadow form morphs and mutates, spasms of darkness burning from the direct light of the electricity and the pain of the shock itself. The acrid stench of sulfur and melted plastic fills the space.

I duck down, clenching my hand into a fist. Blood from my small cut stains my fingers.

"You have a way to contact hell," the leader says in a callous, apathetic voice. "You can bring Satan here so we might make a deal."

I don't know how she speaks through the soft whimpering coming from Skia. Anger spikes like daggers in my heart and head.

Missy trembles beside me. Her back is arched, every hair on end, her eyes nearly slits.

The whimpering turns to panting breaths and then eases to Skia's regular voice. I poke my head back up. Skia is back to the lumpy shadow form, slightly smaller but no longer actually smoking.

"*You want me to contact Satan?*" The incredulity in Skia's tone worries me. I fear what these assholes will do when faced with Skia's rare brand of humor. "*I'm... I'm a sneeze demon, you imbeciles. I've never met the Fallen Angel.*"

There are noises of protest.

Skia cuts across them with a louder, more powerful intrusion into everyone's minds. "*I am of the lowest rank of demon known to hell. I have existed for three thousand years and am considered a* child *by those who serve Lucifer. I barely have one name; he has a thousand.*"

"But surely you can—"

"*You are asking an ant to speak to an elephant. A pebble to move the ocean. A mail boy to demand a consult with the CEO!*"

I stifle a snort at the last one. Something tells me my little shadow friend has been watching office dramas while I do class-work with my noise-canceling headphones on.

The cluster of witches finally seems to get what Skia has been saying. They step away, circling together and muttering in low voices. I know from experience how good Skia's lack-of-ears are.

I take advantage of the witches being distracted and move along the edge of the loft toward the ladder on the side. A plank of wood moans beneath my foot. I freeze, eyes wide as the chatter below halts.

How long has Ags been gone now?

"Who's there?" a voice calls up.

I wince, a shiver going up my spine as a sense of defeat sets in. Missy brushes past my leg, hurrying behind a crate and out of sight.

I try not to breathe.

A rush of air, hot and heavy and stinking of sage, swirls around me. The breath in my lungs eases out between my lips without my permission. I feel hollow. Empty. I cannot draw a fresh breath.

My hands clench and unclench. I take a few staggering steps toward the edge of the loft. My vision begins to blur and fear sets in.

"*Stop.*"

Skia's hiss is a desperate, angry sound.

The spell breaks. I can breathe again, though pain still lingers in my chest.

"Come down." I recognize the blonde's voice.

"Yes," one of the others says. "Come down so we can see you before we kill you."

I swallow. My not-cut palm rubs small circles over the center of my chest, trying to send away the thick hurt. "All right," I call. "I'm coming down."

Descending the ladder with my back to the witches is *not* ideal. But I do it. When I turn at the bottom, a flush fills my cheeks. The heat of anger, embarrassment, and fear paints my face red.

I'm only a few yards from the witches, the sigil, and Skia. Up close, their little black form is trembling.

"Are you okay?" I ask them directly, ignoring the cloaked women. Two of them stay near my friend. The other two hold different artifacts Ags could probably identify. The only one I recognize is the smoking bundle of sage.

Good to know they require items for their spells. The thought of someone being able to pull the air from my lungs like that any time they want is terrifying.

Skia snorts. A little plume of shadow dissipates above them. *"Not nearly. These Morgana wannabees have been using magic, Demi."*

"I know." I take a step toward them, but the witches holding spell ingredients close in between us, blocking my path.

"Of course, we have." The tallest of the witches, a pale woman with straight black hair, removes her hood. She gives me half of a cursory glance, before facing Skia. "You are a powerful being. Pretending otherwise is a lie."

I swallow. The two witches who cast a spell on me—one of whom is the barista—keep their gazes trained on me. The others ignore me.

"They can't use their power," I cut in as the blonde opens her mouth again. "It's too dangerous."

"Ahh, so it has used power before?"

My lip curls. "*They* have, yes. And were nearly dragged back to hell for it."

To my horror, the witches light up with excitement. The blonde grins, glancing at her companions before crouching beside Skia.

"Excellent. You use some power, and we get a gate to hell."

Eight

"That's a really bad idea." Fear runs like beads of ice through my veins.

"Why?" The witch doesn't look my way.

Her fellows seem to have lost interest in me as well. Some of my pride suffers at the thought that they don't see me as any level of threat at all.

I answer her question anyway. "You have no idea what kind of forces you're dealing with. The *thing* that came to collect them last time nearly killed us. It won't have any interest in making deals with you."

"Maybe not before." The barista places her items on the side of a tractor. She flexes her hands.

My eyes widen at how dark her veins are. What should be pale blue lines just under her flesh are dark blue. They protrude from the skin, like miniature ridged mountains.

She meets my gaze, a wicked smile splitting her lips. "Things are different. There was a shift."

The lust for power in her eyes makes me wish I'd brought some sort of weapon. Who knows what would work against these people. But anything in my hand right now would make me feel less helpless.

"There was a change," the blonde says. She stands, briefly caressing the golden cage.

Skia flinches away from her fingers.

"Surely you felt it?" The pale witch raises an eyebrow. Her voice is ghostly and ethereal. The greed behind her words is unsettling.

"I don't know what you're talking about," I mutter. My mind whirls. These women are crazy. Clinically insane with strange magic to back up their disturbing plans. They need a medical facility. Therapy. Something.

Ags has to have been gone long enough by now. But without me to text her which plan to go with...

I take half a step closer to Skia. At the very least, maybe I can smash the cage. If Skia is free they can get outside, get to Ags. Get safe.

Almost as though they can hear my thoughts, a pair of little red eyes fix on me. Skia speaks, and though it's not *technically* using their demonic power they do use some of their own dwindling energy to make sure I'm the only one who can hear them.

"You have to get out of here, Demi. They're dangerous. I don't want them to hurt you."

At the same time, three of the witches encroach upon me.

"You had to feel it."

"The change in the air."

"Impossible became possible."

"Hypothetical became real."

Their voices are hypnotic and disturbed. Only the blonde remains quiet, watching me. I meet her eye, choosing not to look at the ones closing in on me even though every instinct tells me to keep my attention on them.

"Why do this?" My voice is steady. I think my anger has hit a threshold beyond fear. "You clearly have magic. Do you really need more?"

"There is never enough." The low tone of her voice, the glint in her eye, and the determination in the set of her jaw pull a touch of pity from me.

"That sounds like a sad way to live."

The witches pounce.

Two grab my arms. I wrench away from their grasps, but the third uses that damn magic again. It's not as strong—maybe because only one is doing it. But I still choke on the air in my throat.

I grit my teeth and swing my clenched fist. My knuckles impact the barista's cheek. She gasps, fury and disbelief etched across her face.

I shake my stinging hand, a few drops of blood darkening the hay beneath my feet. My act of rebellion infuriates them; the two not holding the spell snatch hold of me again, their fingers gripping like talons against my skin.

The lack of oxygen takes the fight out of me. At least for now.

I focus on dragging air into my lungs, doubled over as my vision starts going dark again. It's like breathing through a thin straw.

Vaguely, as though across a crowded room, I catch the blonde witch's words. She directs them at Skia.

"Give us what we want, demon. Or your friend dies."

"*Please. Let them go. I'll...*" The strain in Skia's voice hurts more than the lack of oxygen. "*I'll do it. I'll use my power. Just let them go.*"

The air returns to me, and I stagger forward at the sudden full breath in my chest. I stare at Skia. Memories flash through my mind. The fear in their voice when we faced Nexus. Their willingness to sacrifice themselves back then as well, when we'd barely known each other. When my kindness was an alien concept to them.

The thought of Skia going back to a place where kindness is weakness, friendship is foolishness, and love is nonexistent fills me with an entirely different kind of sadness.

"Skia..." I murmur, meeting that red gaze.

"We will release them when a gate opens. No sooner. Your kind is devious. We are not fools."

A scoff dies in my throat as a new sound catches my attention. The witches notice as well. The blonde holds up a hand, looking from Skia to the barn door.

A rushing sound comes from outside. Wind, roaring and whipping though no part of the building shakes. Moaning, deep and guttural. Hissing, sharper than Skia's with occasional foreign words making their way through the noise.

"Well done." The blonde grins down at Skia. She looks to the barista witch. "Go, see if there is a way through."

With the witches' attention on the door they don't notice Missy prowling toward Skia's cage. Skia, for their part, doesn't correct the witch. I wonder how far away Ags parked. If the soundtrack she found will have something to give us away, or if it will loop and they'll figure it out.

Then again, the second the barista witch sees a parked car, windows rolled down, blasting haunted sounds found on YouTube, the jig is up.

Which means we need to move fast.

Nine

I move backwards, slow steps as the witches approach the barn door with all the greed of a Wall Street bro glinting in their eyes. We—Missy and I—need to get Skia out of that cage, get to a door, and get to Ags. The car will be ready to go, I hope.

The witches don't have a way to track us, I hope.

They won't follow us all the way to the wedding, I hope.

There is too much hope in this plan and not nearly enough guarantee.

Missy has claws out scratching at the ground. The sigil. She's disrupting the paint. Smart kitty.

I get a few feet from Skia when the blonde witch notices me.

"Stop," she snaps. But she moved toward the barn door too. She's a few feet away.

I lunge.

My fingers latch around the thin metal of the golden cage, and I heft it. Knowing the force won't—shouldn't—hurt Skia, I hurl the thing as hard as I can.

Golden lines crack and splinter as the cage slams into concrete.

It breaks apart at the same time that the sounds from outside stop. The barista bursts back through the door, fury etches across her face.

"It was a trick," she spits.

But the blonde already knows this. She works her fingers, twisting her hands and muttering.

The sigil on the ground lights up. Red glows across the lines. Missy yowls and darts back. I frantically look from the sigil beneath my feet to the witch. She gives a wicked grin. My heart takes up an irregular beat. The blood in my veins warms to an uncomfortable level.

The sigil sputters. The red light hits scratch marks through the paint and falters. With a sound like a sputtering teapot removed from the stove, the paint returns to black.

The grin drops from the witch's face. Her lips twist into a furious scowl. "You can't keep this kind of power all to yourself."

I wince as she raises her hands again.

A familiar voice calls from behind me, at the back of the barn. "Only your kind tries to keep power to yourself. The rest of us share."

A flash of relief is quickly followed by worry as the witches turn their focus on Ags. My wiccan friend steps from the shadows. Her hands are raised, fingers decked with rings and some sort of pattern inked onto her palms with what looks like sharpie.

"Your greed will be your downfall. Those of us who understand and value community will only continue to grow."

The blonde woman scoffs. "*Strigas*," she hollers, calling the other witches to her side.

They hurry forward, pulling items from their cloaks and casting as one.

Fear clutches my chest. We need to run.

I look to the shattered cage, but there is no sign of Skia. Good, they got out.

Missy is moving toward Ags. I dart toward her, scooping as I go and shifting her in my arms until she gets in a sturdy position on my shoulder. When I reach Ags' side the air is already sparking with whatever dark magic the witches are setting into motion.

"We have to—" My voice fails me. I double over. Every exposed bit of flesh feels as though it's being burned.

Agatha keeps her gaze on the witches. "Take hold of my arm."

I do as she says. The burning eases. Not gone but lessened by whatever protective magic Ags has.

"What are we going to do?" I mutter.

My plan went as far as run-out-the-door. If they hadn't been torturing Skia, maybe I would have had time to come up with something better. As it is, I'm worried my little friend won't have enough shadow left to make it to the car without protection from the sun.

"Step back, slowly."

Ags' voice is already strained. Sweat beads along her forehead, and she's swaying slightly. The air warps around us, those little sparks unable to fully penetrate the field of goodness Ags gives off.

"You won't make it to the door." The blonde witch stops her chanting to taunt us. Flanking her, the others keep it up, their whole focus on the spell. "We're going to kill you, find your demon friend, and force it to give us what we want. You shouldn't have gotten involved."

"But that's what friends do."

Skia's voice, distorted and deep, sounds from above, and everyone looks up. A shadow of darkness sits tucked into the corner of a rafter, red eyes glowing down at the witches.

Realization slams into me as my demonic friend drifts away from their perch. I turn, grabbing Ags by the shoulder and forcing her around. With our backs to the witches, we can't see exactly what Skia does. But the screams conjure enough to the imagination that I'm glad I'm not watching.

I walk us forward, Ags leaning on me hard as we make our way to the rear door. The screams stop after a few seconds. I don't let us look back.

We get through the door. Light pours over us. The sun has risen.

"Go," I say, leaning in so Missy can get to Ags' shoulder. "Get to the car. We'll be right there."

"Demi—"

"Go."

Ags, leaning hard on the exterior wall of the barn, heeds my words.

I watch her go, blinking in the bright light. Then I take a deep breath, square my shoulders, and hurry back into the barn.

Ten

The center of the barn is no longer concrete. Red and orange molten edges ring an eight-foot-wide pit of darkness that is worse than any sort of gate to hell my imagination could have created. The witches stand at the four cardinal directions.

Floating above the black is a shadow that is far too small. Skia seems to have shrunk by half with the use of their power. They're barely bigger than Missy's head.

I don't think they're the one who opened the pit.

Their effect on the witches is evident in the black oozing from the women's eyes, ears, and noses. They stand frozen, eyes wide with horror either at what Skia did or the consequences of demonic power.

There is barely time to contemplate which.

Spindly legs, some scaled, some coated in peach fuzz, and some spiked, reach up through the opening.

I take a few steps back, my heartbeat thundering in my ears.

The blonde witch vibrates where she stands. With a grunt of effort that sends another rush of black ooze from her nostrils, she breaks free of Skia's power.

"Great forces of darkness," she calls, her eyes alight with excitement. "We come to you for a deal. Our abilities have grown great, but we know there is much, much more. Let the Coven of Striga serve you."

My stomach roils at the stench of sulfur emanating from the pit. Smoke seeps out, tendrils of it wrapping around the legs of the witches on all four sides.

"WE NEED NOTHING FROM YOU."

Every instinct in my flinches at the voice coming from below.

A long strand of smoke reaches toward Skia.

"BUT IF YOU WOULD GIVE YOUR SOULS SO WILLINGLY..."

I suck in a breath through pursed lips. "This is nuts." I step back again, giving myself room for the insanity I'm about to attempt.

The strands of black tighten around the witches' legs.

I grit my teeth and sprint straight toward the pit.

The acrid air stings my lungs. I heave thick breaths, fear pushed aside as that strand reaching for Skia makes contact with my shadowy friend.

My foot reaches the edge. I leap.

Heat pummels my skin. I don't look down. Don't want to see what is in that hellish chasm. My sight is set on Skia. I reach, scooping like I've done so many times these past few months that Skia has been part of our little family.

Barely any weight, but enough to reassure me that I have them, settles in my arms.

We slam to the ground on the far side of the pit. I roll, pain thudding through my shoulder and hip on the side where I landed.

With Skia still firmly clenched in my arms, I dash the short distance to the door and race into the waiting sunlight.

· · · · ● · ● · · · ·

"What about Nexus?" Ags asks anxiously. Her hair is a frizzy mess from how many times she's ran her ringed hands through it. She shoots a glance behind us.

I exhale and look in the rearview mirror. We've left Salem behind. The highway is ahead, the Atlantic Ocean to our right as we make our way north. Should be at the wedding venue by late afternoon. Not as early as planned, but with plenty of time to help set up before tomorrow.

A chuckle escapes me. A mix of incredulity that I'm even thinking about the wedding right now, and a bit of the leftover fear that needs a way out of my body.

"What?" Ags demands.

I shake my head, concentrating back on the road. "I don't think we need to worry about that right now. Whatever was coming out of that pit didn't look like Nexus."

"Most demons have been gone from this plane for a long time. I doubt Nexus, or any others who may emerge to find me, can track us at this speed."

I glance at the odometer with a raised eyebrow. "Seventy?"

"Horse and carriage, Demi. That is what my kind is used to."

"I guess that makes sense," Ags says, a bit of relief in her tone. She strokes Missy, currently settled comfortably in her lap.

"And you, pretty little miss." Ags shoots me a glance. "I'm very curious about exactly how intelligent she is now."

I nod at the same time that Missy lets out a little mew. "Don't worry, Missy. We won't have you doing tricks for treats. We know you're not a dog."

The joke is offset by a satisfied sounding purr. Ags lets out a tight chuckle.

I adjust the sweater draped over my legs and take a peek at Skia. They're huddled below, out of the way of the car pedals but still brushing against my calves. Concern stirs in my stomach at how small they are after everything that happened.

Then again, we haven't eaten anything. I tighten my grip on the steering wheel.

"I want to go a few more hours before we stop to eat, but we should get food soon."

"*Agreed,*" Skia hisses. "*My form has shrunk considerably. A bowl of fries. Or perhaps a brownie. Ice cream...*"

They continue on like that for a while. Ags laughs, the tension in her shoulders loosening at Skia's lack of worry.

I can't quite get past the nerves bunched in my gut. There are too many unanswered questions. And that voice, deep and terrifying and unworldly, still rings through my ears when the car gets too quiet.

Part of me wants to know what became of those witches. Part of me never wants to find out. And another part of me is viciously glad for whatever horrible fate awaits them. They deserve it for hurting Skia.

• • • ●•●• • •

Agatha's cousin, Stacey, isn't bothered at all by our lateness. She and her partner, an ex-Navy man the size of a tree trunk, are all laughs and smiles. I'm reluctant to risk anyone seeing Skia, but that becomes a non-issue when the soon-to-be newlyweds show us a pair of adjoined rooms at the cottage-style hotel where the wedding is going to happen.

We unpack, and I leave Skia in the room with Missy. The curtains are drawn, the lights are off, a box of pizza is open on the bed, and New Girl is playing on my laptop.

Set up is fun, even with my bruised shoulder and the bandage on my hand. These are the kind of people who enjoy the wanderlust, whimsical side of life. We line the ceremony arch with moss, mushrooms, fairy lights, and ceramic butterfly wings. The weather should hold, so setting out the benches and decorative flowers early isn't an issue.

Stacey and Tyler don't even mind when I excuse myself as the night-before party gets going.

I can't stand the thought of being away from Skia longer than necessary. And I'm utterly exhausted.

I gobble down the last slice of cold pizza when I return to the room, give Missy a few scritches behind her ear, and lay down next to Skia.

In the darkness, only their glowing red eyes are visible.

"*What is wrong, Demi?*"

I huff out a laugh. "I mean, this morning wasn't exactly my idea of a fun stop on a road trip."

They are silent for a minute.

I shift, leaning on my elbow to look at them. "They hurt you."

"*They did.*"

"I'm sorry."

"*Nothing that happened this morning was your fault, Demi. Except our escape. If you hadn't done what you did, I'd be a minuscule ball of darkness, fading away in that cage. Or I'd be sucked back to that infernal place.*" They shudder.

"I wouldn't let that happen." My voice is strained; the knowledge that it's not as simple as that is very present in my mind.

Skia clearly thinks the same, as a low hissing laugh reverberates through my head. After a moment the laughter ceases. "*It was… unsettling to see magic of that nature in the world again.*"

"Again?"

"*It was prevalent at one time. Long, long ago. Before I was allowed on this plane the first time.*"

I sit with that for some time. "Is there anything we can do about it? Are we safe now those witches are gone?"

Skia snorts. "*The Coven of Striga? A rather obvious name, by the way. And no. I don't believe this business of demonic power available to humans is done.*"

I nod, weariness dragging at me. This feels too big for the amount of energy left in my body. I lay my head back on the pillow. "Sounds like a tomorrow problem."

"*Of course, there certainly isn't anything to be done about it tonight.*"

My voice is muffled as I turn and cradle the pillow under my head. "We're safe though, right? No more paralysis in the dead of night? No pits to hell?"

"We're safe, Demi. I'm keeping my senses active now I know what threats lurk on this plane. That pit closed up not long after we got away."

"You can know that?" Sleepiness pulls my eyes closed.

"I can know that. It will mean consuming more of your scones to keep up my energy. But there are a handful of things I can do without calling on the forces of hell."

"Good, good."

Skia's shadowy shape, a little heavier after downing nearly a whole pizza, settles into the crook of my arm, pressed against me like a comfort plushy. On the other side, Missy does the same.

· · · ● · ● · ● · ● · · ·

The wedding is gorgeous. Stacey is a vision in her lacey gown, violet and white flowers woven through the train and her hair. Tyler is in his military uniform, a stark contrast to the rest of the union, but a dashing visage all the same.

I look pretty dang good myself. This is the first time I've ever felt comfortable at a wedding. Not forced into what my family thought was appropriate, but wearing something that makes me happy.

Agatha wears her signature black and purple. Ruffled sleeves hang low as she pulls forth the vows. Her voice carries to the back of the bench seating, clear and purposeful. It seems to move every attendee to sit a little straighter. Soft wind blows through the trees around us and, as the bride and groom exchange a kiss a cascade of lavender colored petals descend over us all.

Where they came from is a question only I am asking, as none of the trees near us are flowering and no one threw them.

My lip twitches into a smile as Ags gently touches the newlyweds' shoulders before they head down the aisle.

A spark of gold lingers where her fingers landed, and my smile grows.

Thank you so much for coming on another Spooky Cat story;
I hope you've enjoyed the ride.

Please consider leaving a review if you like the story.

For more from C.H. Lyn, visit chlyn.com.